Day Travelcard

OFF-PEAK
Route ANY PERMITTED
CHILD

THANK YOU
PLEASE RETAIN FOR YOUR RECORDS
Not for resale

AUTH: 021882 TIME: 8:52

RETURN TICKET

I ♥ Picnics

BERLIN
Rome
MADRID
OSLO
PARIS

BEGINNER'S GUIDE -TO- deep sea diving

JUNGLE SAFARI
PLEASE DO NOT FEED THE ANIMALS

D0413201

First published in 2014 by Child's Play (International) Ltd
Ashworth Road, Bridgemead, Swindon SN5 7YD UK

Published in USA by Child's Play Inc.
250 Minot Avenue, Auburn, Maine 04210

Distributed in Australia by Child's Play Australia Pty Ltd
Unit 10/20 Narabang Way, Belrose, NSW 2085

Text and illustrations copyright © 2014 Gillian Hibbs
The moral right of the author and illustrator has been asserted

ISBN 978-1-84643-596-6

CLP121113CPL12135966

Printed and bound in Shenzhen, China

1 3 5 7 9 10 8 6 4 2

A catalogue record of this book is available from the British Library

www.childs-play.com

Tilly's
At Home
Holiday

Gillian Hibbs

"Why can't **we** go on holiday?" asked Tilly.

"Tariq is going to India,

Paris is going to Paris,

and Tim is going camping."

Rory is going to the seaside,

Chanel is going to Spain,

"We'll have just as much
fun as everyone else, you'll see,"
Mum answered. "Maybe more!"

That night, Tilly went to have tea with Paris. Her mum was packing a huge suitcase full of all the things they needed for their holiday.

Back home, Tilly had
a sneaky look to see if Mum
was packing the old suitcase
they sometimes took to visit Granny.
It was sitting on top of the chest of
drawers gathering dust, just like it always did.

The next day,
Tilly walked home from
school with Tariq and his dad.
"Who's he talking to?" whispered Tilly.
"The travel agent," replied Tariq.
"He's sorting out the flights for tomorrow."

At home, the phone rang.

"Hello Granny,"
Tilly sighed disappointedly.
"I thought you might have been
the travel agent."

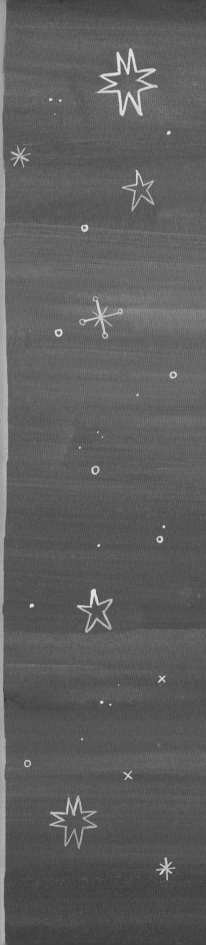

Tilly was really down in the dumps.
"It's the holidays and I'm not
doing anything at all!" she sniffed.
But she couldn't help hoping that

**something exciting might
be about to happen,**

and went to sleep with
a little tingle in her toes.

The next morning, Tilly was allowed to have breakfast in Mum's bed, just like she did on her birthday!

"Get your best adventuring clothes on,
My Little Explorer," Mum smiled.
"We've got a bus to catch!"

BUS STOP

When they got off the bus, Tilly was puzzled.
"Why have you brought me to the library?" she asked.

SPACE

KINGS AND QUEENS

UNICORNS

PENGUINS

It was a hot day outside, but the library
was cool, breezy and peaceful.

Mum told Tilly stories of faraway places and marvellous people. They were worlds away...

...fighting dragons,
sailing pirate ships,
meeting princesses...

TO THE PARK →

...and hiding from **ferocious beasts.**

Then it was time to stop for a well-earned lunch in a Top Secret Hideaway...

TO THE SWIMMING POOL

...before discovering
hidden treasure and rare sea creatures.

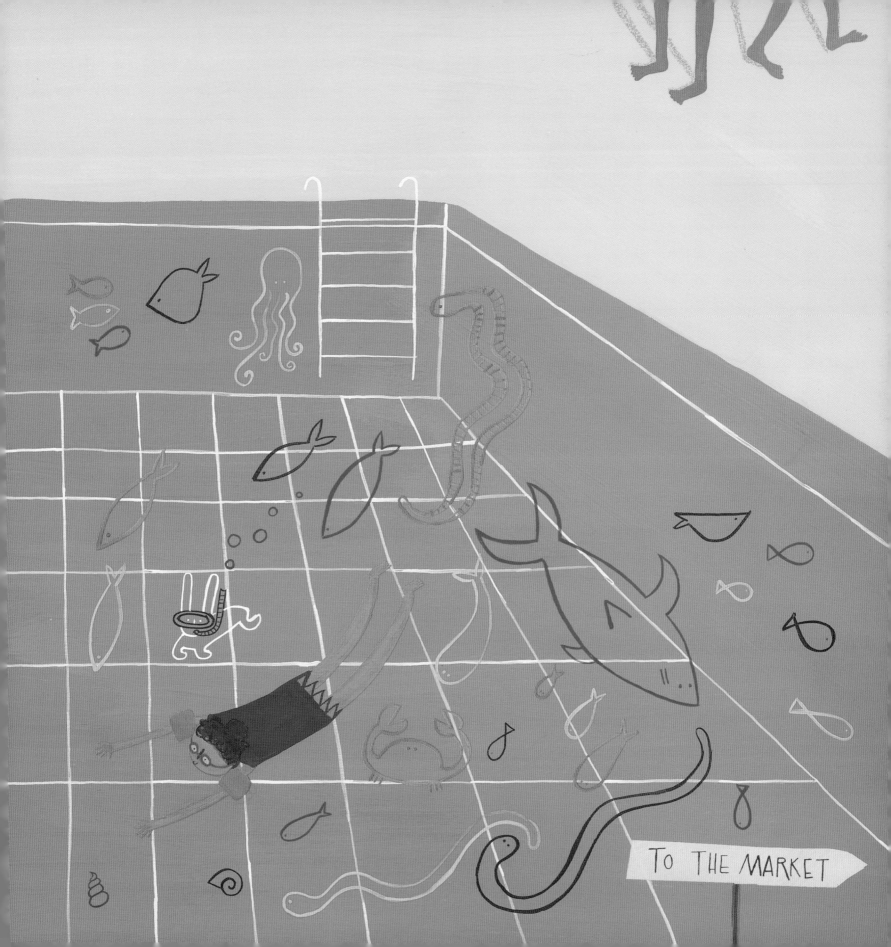

TO THE MARKET

At the market, they found

a mermaid's mirror, a genie's lamp and golden coins from distant lands.

How had they ended up here?

When they got home,
Tilly was tired.
"I've got an idea!" said Mum.

"Run around

the flat

and collect

all the

sheets,

towels

and

blankets

you can find."

"Ta da!" Mum had made the most beautiful tent that Tilly had ever seen.

"Welcome to **our holiday home!**" laughed Mum.

Inside the **tent,**

they told **stories** all night.

Tilly was so happy.
It had been a **wonderful** adventure.

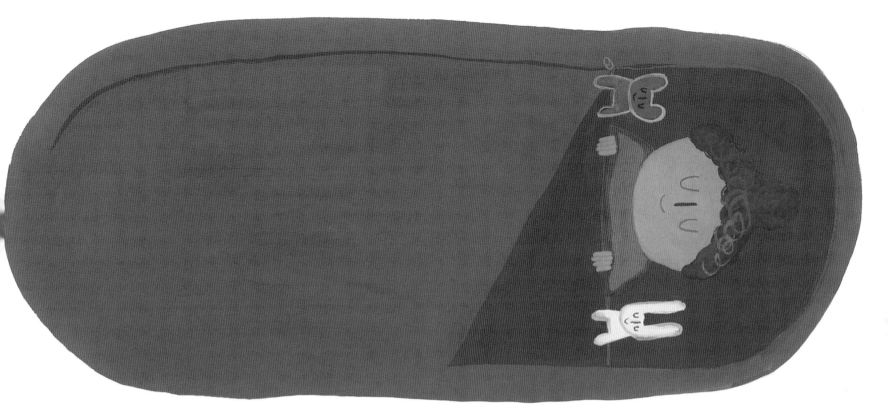

"I can't wait to tell my friends about **my stay-at-home holiday!**"

And she did!